WITHDRAWN

My Brother, My Sister, and Me

A FIRST LOOK AT SIBLING RIVALRY

PAT THOMAS
ILLUSTRATED BY LESLEY HARKER

BARRON'S

Do you have a brother or sister?
Do you sometimes wish that
you didn't?

Do you ever imagine how nice it would be if you were the only child in your family?

Everyone who has a brother or
sister feels this way sometimes.

Especially when they follow you around without being asked or draw pictures in your favorite book.

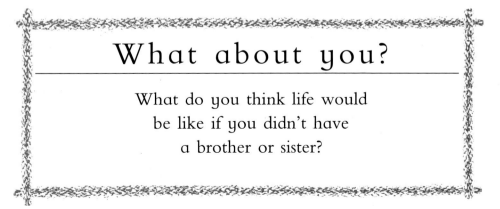

What about you?

What do you think life would
be like if you didn't have
a brother or sister?

When you have a brother or sister
it may feel like you never
get the right sort
of attention.

Either you
don't get noticed
when you've done
something good or you
get noticed too often when
you do something naughty.

It can be hard to like your brother or sister when you think that your parents love them more or that they are better at everything than you are.

But everybody is special. Each person has things that they are good at and things they are bad at.

What about you?

Do you ever wish you were more like your brother or sister? What things are you good at?

When you're feeling unhappy about
having a brother or sister the last thing
you feel like doing is sharing with them.

But in families everybody
has to learn to share.

The bigger your family is, the more you will
have to learn to share things like toys, the
television, and your parents' attention.

Sharing can be hard. But fighting is even harder. It is terrible to live in a house where children are always fighting and competing with each other.

Often parents don't know what to do to
make things peaceful again.

It is hard for them to be fair to each of you
every minute of every day.

Even though
having a brother
or sister can be hard
work, it can also be fun
because it means you can have
more of lots of good things.

After all, there is more
chance that someone
will be there to play
with you and teach
you new games.

When you have a brother or sister you
always have someone to share secrets with
or share chores with.

There are more people in the house
to love and take care of you.

When you have a nightmare, your brother or sister may be the first one there to chase the monsters away. At school, they may protect you from bullies.

What about you?

Do you enjoy sharing with your brother or sister?
What kinds of things do you do together?

All families need to learn how to get along with each other. Everyone has to keep practicing being fair and sharing with others—even parents.

You don't all have to be the same, look the same, or like the same things to like each other. In fact, families can be a lot more interesting when all are allowed to be themselves.

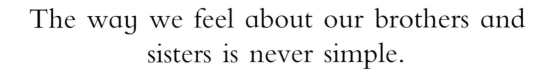

The way we feel about our brothers and sisters is never simple.

Even when
you are grown up
it is sometimes hard
to understand how you
feel about them.

Some grown-ups still feel that they have to compete with their brothers and sisters.

This can make them very unhappy. That's why it's best to learn how to get along right from the start.

The important thing to remember is that even though you fight sometimes, that doesn't mean you have stopped loving each other.

And even though you, your brother, and your sister may be very different, your parents love each of you.

HOW TO USE THIS BOOK

The way children feel about their brothers and sisters is very complex. Often they will feel a wide range of emotions long before they are able to say what those emotions are. Parents and teachers can help in many ways.

Here are some simple guidelines.

Try to avoid comparing one child with another. When you do this you lock your children into roles that they may never get out of (for example, the good one, the naughty one). Instead it is important to respect the differences between your children and affirm that these differences are all right with you.

Sometimes even sensitive parents allow insensitive things to happen between their children. You can't always get it right, so don't be too hard on yourself. Instead, focus on what you might do differently next time.

Parents can sometimes contribute to sibling rivalry. It is a family problem, not a problem that exists only between children. How you handle your children's arguing may reflect what you experienced in your own childhood. Make sure it reflects it in a positive way. If you are doing the same negative things to your children that your parents did to you, now is the time to break that pattern.

Teachers need to be aware of not making comparisons between siblings, but to encourage the individuality of each child at every stage of development. An eye-opening project about fantasies and expectations within families is to have children with brothers and sisters write about what life would be like without their siblings, and have only-children write about what life would be like with a sibling. Then compare responses in class and use them to promote lively discussion.

Try to get past the idea that your children should be great friends. Friendship is based on similarities. Sibling relationships, by their very nature, are based on differences. A better goal is to help your children develop the skills to get along with other people—to learn to respect differences, resolve difficulties, and develop a caring relationship. These skills will support them through all of their lives.

Alternatively, for older children, a family-tree exercise is useful to help children see that nobody is perfect and each of us is different. Children can be encouraged to list the best and worst qualities of everyone in the family (including themselves).

BOOKS TO READ

For Children

The Berenstain Bears and the Green-Eyed Monster
Stan and Jan Berenstain (Random House, 1995)

Just Me and My Little Brother
Mercer Meyer (Golden Books, 1991)

For Adults

Sibling Rivalry
Seymor Reit (Ballantine, 1985)

Siblings Without Rivalry
Adele Faber and Elaine Mazlish (Avon, 1988)

Loving Each One Best
Nancy Samalin with Catherine Whitney (Bantam, 1997)

USEFUL CONTACT

Parents Anonymous
675 West Foothill Blvd.
Suite 220
Claremont, CA 91711-3416
(909) 621-6184
*Believes that all parents experience problems at some time,
and that all deserve help. Maintains support groups, along
with self-help development programs.*